OLIVIA
Says Good Night

by Gabe Pulliam and Farrah McDoogle
illustrated by Patrick Spaziante

Simon Spotlight
New York   London   Toronto   Sydney   New Delhi

Based on the TV series OLIVIA™ as seen on Nickelodeon™

SIMON SPOTLIGHT
An imprint of Simon & Schuster Children's Publishing Division
1230 Avenue of the Americas, New York, New York 10020
This Simon Spotlight paperback edition September 2016
OLIVIA™ Ian Falconer Ink Unlimited, Inc. and © 2011 Ian Falconer and Classic Media, LLC.
Also available in a Simon Spotlight hardcover edition
All rights reserved, including the right of reproduction in whole or in part in any form.
SIMON SPOTLIGHT and colophon are registered trademarks of Simon & Schuster, Inc.
For information about special discounts for bulk purchases, please contact Simon & Schuster Special Sales
at 1-866-506-1949 or business@simonandschuster.com.
Manufactured in the United States of America 0816 LAK
1 2 3 4 5 6 7 8 9 10
ISBN 978-1-4814-6817-6 (pbk)
ISBN 978-1-4424-2947-5 (deluxe POB)
ISBN 978-1-4424-4665-6 (eBook)

One evening, a little while before bedtime, Olivia was reading a story to Ian. It was a wonderful story about a princess who had an adventure in the desert.

"The best part was when they built that beautiful tent," said Olivia as she finished the story.

"That was my favorite part too," agreed Ian.

"But there should have been robots!"

Olivia imagined what it would be like to live in a beautiful tent in the desert, just like the princess in the story.
"I wonder . . ."

"Where do you want all this treasure?" Prince Ian asked.
"Over by my dresses, please!" said Princess Olivia.

"Ian, I have an amazing idea!" Olivia said excitedly. Just as Olivia was about to tell Ian her idea, Mom came in. "It's getting late," she said. "Please start cleaning up and then get ready for bed."

"I guess your amazing idea will have to wait until tomorrow," said Ian.
"No, it won't," replied Olivia. "We're going to build a tent in my room, just like the one in the story! We can clean up and build at the same time!"
"We can?" asked Ian.

Under Olivia's expert direction, they got right to work. "All right, Ian," said Olivia, "Toys go in the trunk . . . books on the shelf . . . and everything we need for our tent can go on the bed."

Before they knew it, the room was clean!
As Olivia was putting some last things away
in her trunk, she saw exactly what she needed
to finish the tent.

"Your room looks great," said Ian.
Olivia pulled the blanket from her bed. She draped it to make a flap door, just like on a real tent.
"Hmm . . . it needs one more thing," Olivia noted as she added a glittery red O to the flap door.
"Awesome!" exclaimed Ian.

Olivia and Ian were putting the finishing touches on the tent when Mom called from the hallway. "It's time for bed, Ian," she said, "and, Olivia, it's bath time for you, and then bedtime." "Don't worry, Ian. You can play in the tent tomorrow," said Olivia.

As Olivia settled into her warm and sudsy bath, she remembered that every tent needs treasure, and where better to find treasure than the bottom of the sea? She imagined what it would be like to be a scuba diver exploring for treasure. "I wonder . . ."

A pod of seals were all pointing their flippers in the same direction.
"Jewels? Over there?" Olivia asked them, and they nodded their heads. "I have a
way with animals," Olivia said as she swam that way. And then she spotted it . . .
a huge treasure chest overflowing with glittering jewels!

"This treasure will be perfect—perfectly perfect!" Olivia thought happily.

Olivia collected the treasures she had found in the bathtub and took them back to her room. She started to put her treasure away when Mom walked by. She had just finished tucking Ian into bed. "I'll be right there, Olivia," she called. "Don't forget your pajamas!"

"These pajamas are pretty good, but I need something extra special to wear inside my tent," Olivia decided. She remembered the flowing gown the princess in the story had been wearing.

"I know!" Olivia exclaimed. She dug through her trunk until she found what she was looking for . . . the scarf Grandma had given her!

"So glamorous!" she declared.

"All right, Olivia, time for bed!" said Mom when she came into Olivia's room.
"But, Mom, I just finished building the most spectacular, super-duper tent ever!"
Olivia protested.

Mom looked around Olivia's room, which was all cleaned up. Then she saw Olivia's tent and was amazed. "That is a beautiful tent," Mom said. "Great job!"

"Ian helped!" Olivia reminded her.

"But it's missing something," said Mom.

"It is?" Olivia exclaimed. *What could possibly be missing?* she wondered.

"Your tent is missing a beautiful girl sleeping inside!" Mom explained. Olivia settled inside and Mom tucked her in.

"Good night, Olivia," Mom said.

"But I can't sleep yet!" Olivia said with a yawn. "There's still so much to do. . . ."

Mom smiled and gave her a gentle kiss good night.

When Mom left the room, Olivia sang to herself:

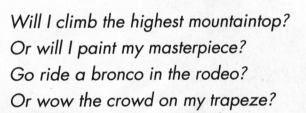

They say "Good night, Olivia.
Your big day is through."
But how can I sleep?
There's still so much to do!

It looks like I'm tucked in tight,
snug in my bed.
But tomorrow is chasing today
through my head.

Will I climb the highest mountaintop?
Or will I paint my masterpiece?
Go ride a bronco in the rodeo?
Or wow the crowd on my trapeze?

Princess, doctor, author, astronaut!
From jungles dark to oceans deep,
I'll do anything, go anywhere.
Just don't ask me to . . .

go . . . to . . . sleeeeep. . . .